LAYLA and the BOTS

BUILT FOR SPEED

written by
Vicky Fang

illustrated by
Christine Nishiyama

BRANCHES™
SCHOLASTIC INC.

For my friend and mentor, Vincent —VF
To Butterbean, for giving me
a whole new world to draw.— CN

Text copyright © 2020 by Vicky Fang
Illustrations copyright © 2020 by Christine Nishiyama

Library of Congress Cataloging-in-Publication Data

Names: Fang, Vicky, author. | Nishiyama, Christine (Illustrator), illustrator.
Title: Built for speed / by Vicky Fang ; illustrated by Christine Nishiyama.
Description: First edition. | New York : Branches/Scholastic Inc., 2020. |
Series: Layla and the Bots ; 2 | Audience: Ages 5-7. | Audience: Grades
K-1. | Summary: Layla and the Bots are eager for Blossom Valley's upcoming go-kart race, but one racer, Tina, needs their help to build a cart with hand controls and other special features.
Identifiers: LCCN 2019031675 | ISBN 9781338582925 (paperback) |
ISBN 9781338582949 (library binding)
Subjects: CYAC: Contests—Fiction. | Karts (Automobiles)—Fiction. |
Automobile racing—Fiction. | People with disabilities—Fiction. |
Robots—Fiction.
Classification: LCC PZ7.1.F3543 Bui 2020 | DDC [E]—dc23
LC record available at https://lccn.loc.gov/2019031675

10 9 8 7 6 5 4 3 2 1   20 21 22 23 24

Printed in China 62
First edition, August 2020

Illustrated by Christine Nishiyama
Edited by Rachel Matson and Katie Carella
Book design by Maria Mercado

TABLE OF CONTENTS

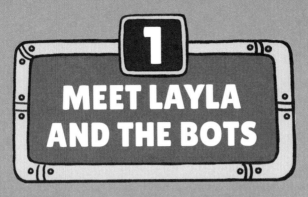

1
MEET LAYLA AND THE BOTS

This is Layla. She is an inventor. And a rock star.

These are the Bots.

BEEP

BOOP

BOP

They are part of Layla's crew.

3

Layla and the Bots play music all
around their town of Blossom Valley.

This week, they are playing at the
go-kart race! That is why they're excited
to learn about things that go FAST . . .

Whenever Layla and the Bots get together, awesome things happen.

2

FAST FRIENDS

On Monday morning, Layla and the Bots
are at the go-kart track. The big race is in
five days—and Layla and the Bots will be
playing at the finish line!

This track is awesome!
Look at those turns!

They check out the go-karts.

BEEP. The town ordered these brand-new go-karts for the race.

Shiny!

So cool.

Other kids start looking at the go-karts, too. But then Layla sees one girl who looks frustrated.

Layla walks over to her.

Hi, I'm Layla.

Hi. I'm Tina.

Is everything okay?

Not really. I'm a great racer!
But these go-karts won't work for me.

Why not?

Tina explains that she has trouble moving her leg muscles.

For example, I can't use the foot pedals in that go-kart.

Hmm. I have an idea . . .

Layla calls the Bots over.

Bots, Tina wants to race. Do you think we can fix up a go-kart for her?

Sounds fun!

Ya-hoo!

Really? I'd love that!

There must be a way Tina can join the race. But what kind of go-kart does she need?

QUICK FIX

Layla and the Bots look over a go-kart with Tina.

How could we make this go-kart work for you?

Tina explains.

I need to control the gas and brake pedals with my hands, not my feet.

Hand controls!

And it'd be great to have an easy way to get in and out by myself.

Easy access.
That makes sense.

Layla and the Bots head to the scrapyard.

On the way, they make a list.

THINGS THAT TINA'S GO-KART WILL NEED:

(1) Hand-operated driving controls

(2) Powered seat that will help her get into and out of the go-kart

They arrive at the scrapyard.
Mayor Diaz is there too! She is
frowning at the piles of junk.

They pile up all the parts they need.

Woo!

We'll have this go-kart up and running in no time. Get ready, Bots! Tomorrow morning, we build!

4

SPEED BUMPS

On Tuesday morning, Layla and the Bots get ready in their workshop. Layla tucks a pencil behind her ear.

Okay, Bots! Time to build.

Beep studies the diagrams.

Boop gathers her tools.

Bop practices handstands while his computers boot up.

First, Beep finds where to add hand controls. They will go on the steering wheel.

Boop connects them to the car.

Bop codes the hand controls to work the gas and the brake.

Then, Beep measures the height for a power seat.

Boop builds the seat.

Bop writes the code to move the seat into the perfect positions for Tina.

position A =
twist left, go up;
position B =
twist right, go down

Great work!

When the go-kart is all hooked up, they are ready to test it out.

Go go go!

Boop starts up the go-kart. She pushes the gas.

The motor growls, but the go-kart doesn't move.

BEEP. Try again!

Layla frowns at the heavy go-kart. It looks like this won't be so simple after all.

Layla and the Bots study the go-kart. Can they figure out a solution?

BEEP. We need all these parts to make the go-kart work for Tina.

This motor is just not strong enough. We need something stronger.

More power.

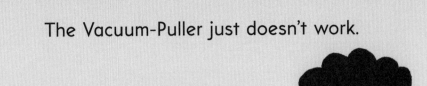

The Vacuum-Puller just doesn't work.

Bah-phooey!

By the end of the day, there is only one idea left. Layla shows the Bots her jetpack diagram.

We attach a jetpack to the back of the go-kart. The power of its blasts will push the go-kart forward!

JETPACK

The Bots see a problem.

BEEP. Your jetpack is strong enough, but the blast is too dangerous.

Yes! What if somebody is behind the go-kart?

Eep, scary!

Layla knows they're right. She sets down the last idea.

> Okay . . . Let's get some rest. We'll figure out how to power this go-kart tomorrow.

Layla worries as she cleans up the workshop. What if they can't help Tina after all?

6

A QUICK BREAK

Early Wednesday morning, Layla wakes up the Bots.

Time to get to work!

I'm too hungry to work.

Layla needs the Bots at their best.
They all walk to the mini-mart to get Boop
a snack.

Everyone waits outside while Boop
goes into the store. Bop practices karate
while he waits.

39

Layla draws up a new plan and shows it to Beep and Bop.

JETPACK WITH MOTION SENSORS

When you hit this button, the sensor will check if there is anything behind the jetpack.

7
JET SET

Layla and the Bots build the jetpack in their workshop.

Okay, Bots. Let's give this go-kart some SPEED!

First, Layla attaches the jetpack.

Next, Boop installs a button on the steering wheel. It will turn on the jetpack.

Beep figures out the right position for the sensor.

Then Bop writes the code to make it all work.

On (button) →
    check sensor
if blocked → don't blast
if not blocked → blast!

It's time to try the jetpack. Everyone moves away from the sensor. Then Beep presses the button.

The boosters blast off!

We did it!

Zippa-dee!

Layla and the Bots bring the new go-kart to Tina at the track.

Tina zooms around the track, blasting the jetpack. The go-kart works perfectly!

She's a great racer!

Super-wow!

So cool!

Mayor Diaz shakes her head.

I'm sorry, but rules are rules. We cannot allow racers to make changes to the go-karts. Everyone needs to drive the same go-kart for it to be a fair race.

Layla is crushed. What are they going to tell Tina?

8

OFF-TRACK

When Tina comes off the track, Layla gives her the bad news.

I'm so sorry. I really thought you would be able to race this go-kart.

Isn't there any way?

A few kids come by. They admire Tina's go-kart. A crowd starts to form.

Did you see how fast this go-kart went?

It is the coolest one I've ever seen!

I wish I had a go-kart <u>this</u> awesome!

Suddenly, Layla has an idea.

She pulls Mayor Diaz aside.

What if you let <u>everybody</u> build a new go-kart? Then it would be a fair race AND we could clean up that mess at the scrapyard!

Mayor Diaz smiles.

That's a great idea!

Racers: We've decided to change the rules. This year we will have Blossom Valley's first <u>scrap-kart</u> race!

Tina's eyes widen.

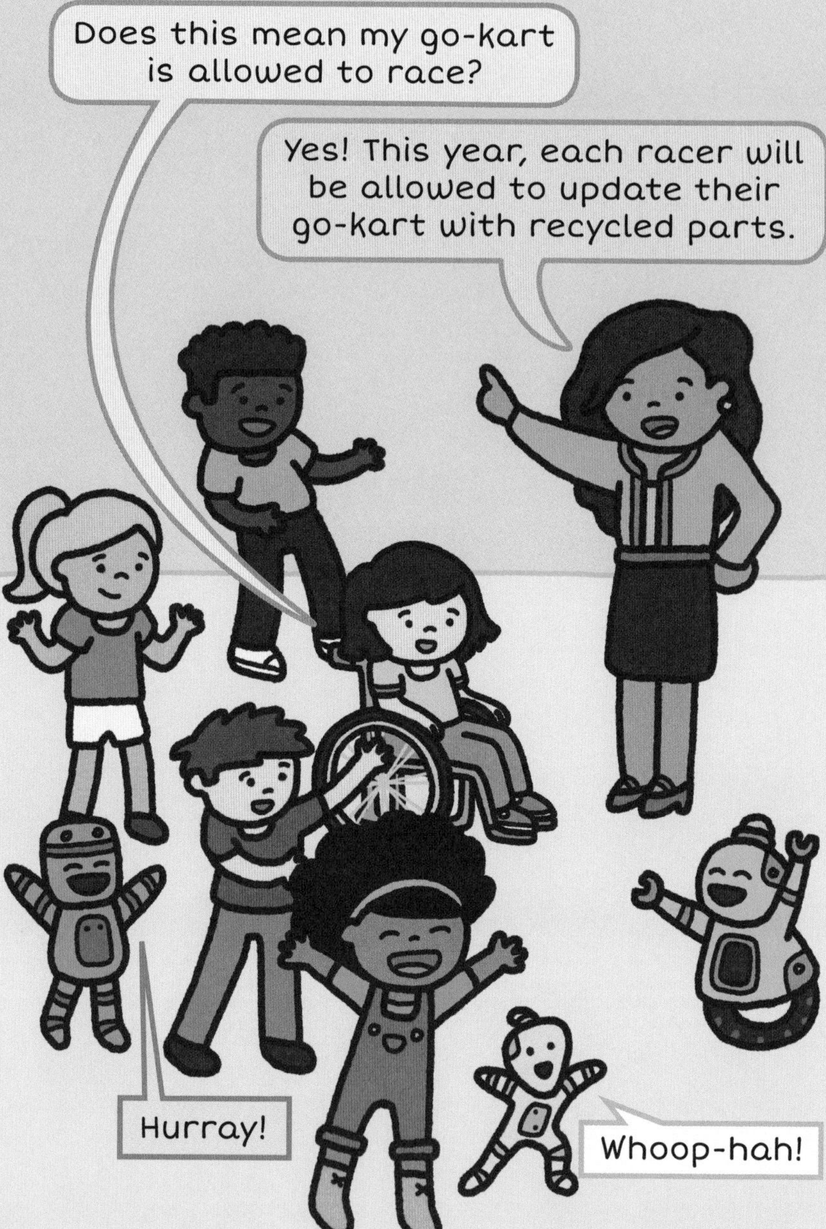

At the scrapyard, Layla and the Bots
help racers pick out parts.

BLOSSOM
VALLEY
SCRAPYARD

Back at their workshop, they tinker and build to help the racers change their go-karts.

These go-karts all look amazing!

By Friday night, every racer has added new parts to their go-kart. Everybody in town is ready for tomorrow's big race!

TAP!
TAP!

9

READY, SET, RACE!

The race is about to begin! Racers are lined up at the starting line.

The racers are off! They zoom around and around the track.

In the final lap, Tina is in second place!

Tina presses the red button . . . but the jetpack doesn't blast!

Someone's right behind you! He's blocking the sensor!

Tina swerves to get out of the other racer's path. Now, he is off to her side. With nobody in her blast path, Tina presses the button again. The jetpack blasts off! She zooms ahead.

And then . . .

Tina zips forward and wins the race!

Tina did it!

Mayor Diaz hands Tina her trophy.
Tina beams.

It was Layla and the Bots' speediest show ever.

DESIGN AND BUILD YOUR OWN

YOU'LL NEED THE FOLLOWING ITEMS:

- 1 empty juice box, with a straw
- 1 balloon
- Duct tape
- Scissors
- 1 rubber band
- Bathtub filled with water

NOTE: Pull and stretch out the balloon a little before starting your experiment.

STEP 1. BUILD THE BOAT

- Lift the triangular flaps at the top of your juice box. Flatten the top half of the box, leaving the bottom half sticking up. This will be your boat.

STEP 2. BUILD THE ENGINE

rubber band

- Tightly wrap the rubber band around the balloon's opening with the straw inside it. This will hold your balloon and straw together. Now you have a balloon engine!

- Place your balloon engine on top of your boat. The straw end should hang down off the flattened side of the boat.

- Tape the straw to the boat.

tape

BALLOON SPEEDBOAT!

STEP 3. TEST AND FIX

- Using the straw, blow up the balloon. Hold the air in by quickly covering the straw opening with your thumb.

- Place the boat in the tub, with the straw end under the water.

- Let go! Watch your boat zoom through the water.

STEP 4. ROCK OUT!

- Have fun! Experiment with different-sized juice boxes and the amount of air you blow into the balloon to see what changes.

- Give your boat a fun name, and draw a picture of your design.

- Decorate your boat. Try adding new parts to it, like a sail or a rudder. Do these new parts change how your boat moves?

HOW MUCH DO YOU KNOW ABOUT BUILT FOR SPEED?

Reread pages 29 and 30. Why won't Tina's go-kart move? What do Layla and the Bots need to find so they can fix the problem?

Layla and the Bots visit the mini-mart. What idea comes out of this visit? How does this fix the problem with Tina's go-kart?

Why won't Mayor Diaz allow Tina's go-kart to race? How does Layla convince her to change the rules?

Look at the pictures on pages 60 and 61. Each go-kart has been updated with parts from the scrapyard. What three new materials can you find?

Imagine that you get to build your own super go-kart! What would your go-kart look like? How would you give the go-kart its speed? Draw and label a diagram of your go-kart!

ABOUT THE CREATORS

VICKY FANG is a product designer who invents things like cars that talk to each other and robots you can build at home. She's never designed a race car . . . but she did once design a car that would tell you about the things outside your window! Vicky lives in California with her husband and kids. LAYLA AND THE BOTS is her first early chapter book series.

CHRISTINE NISHIYAMA is an artist who draws all kinds of things in her sketchbook. She's passionate about helping others make art and draws comics about  being a new mom. Christine lives in North Carolina with her husband, dog, and teeny baby, Butterbean. Christine is also the author and illustrator of the picture book WE ARE FUNGI.